Sand and Snow

By Ann Ingalls
Illustrated by Chris Vallo

Publishing Credits
Rachelle Cracchiolo, M.S.Ed., *Publisher*
Aubrie Nielsen, M.S.Ed., *EVP of Content Development*
Emily R. Smith, M.A.Ed., *VP of Content Development*
Véronique Bos, *Creative Director*
Dani Neiley, *Associate Editor*
Kevin Pham, *Graphic Designer*

Image Credits
Illustrated by Chris Vallo

Library of Congress Cataloging-in-Publication Data
Names: Ingalls, Ann, author. | Vallo, Chris, illustrator.
Title: Sand and snow / by Ann Ingalls ; illustrated by Chris Vallo.
Description: Huntington Beach, CA : Teacher Created Materials, [2022] | Audience: Grades 2-3. | Summary: ""Sadie and Gus go to visit Grandma at her home in the Mojave Desert. They are excited to explore a new place. But the next day, they wake up to a big surprise!""-- Provided by publisher.
Identifiers: LCCN 2021052862 (print) | LCCN 2021052863 (ebook) | ISBN 9781087601885 (paperback) | ISBN 9781087631936 (ebook)
Subjects: LCSH: Readers (Primary) | LCGFT: Readers (Publications)
Classification: LCC PE1119.2 .I547 2022 (print) | LCC PE1119.2 (ebook) | DDC 428.6/2--dc23/eng/20211109
LC record available at https://lccn.loc.gov/2021052862
LC ebook record available at https://lccn.loc.gov/2021052863"

5482 Argosy Avenue
Huntington Beach, CA 92649
www.tcmpub.com

ISBN 978-1-0876-0188-5
© 2022 Teacher Created Materials, Inc.

This book may not be reproduced or distributed in any way without prior written consent from the publisher.

Printed in Malaysia. THU001.46774

Table of Contents

Chapter One:
  Are We There Yet? 4

Chapter Two:
  Covered in Snow! 12

Chapter Three:
  Building a Snowman 18

Chapter Four:
  A Crazy Dream 22

About Us 28

Chapter One

Are We There Yet?

"Are we there yet?" asked Gus.

"Not yet," said Dad. "We will be there soon."

Sadie and Gus could hardly wait! Dad was taking them to see Grandma at her home in the desert. They had never been there. On the way, Sadie sketched with her colored pencils.

"What kind of tree is that, Dad?" asked Sadie, pointing out the window.

"That is a Joshua tree. It only grows in the Mojave Desert."

"Look at those spiky leaves." Sadie picked up her green and brown pencils and sketched the tree.

Then, Gus asked again, "Are we there yet?"

"We'll be there very soon," said Dad.

By the time they got to Grandma's house, the sun was setting.

"Look at those colors!" said Sadie as they got out of the car. "That is the most beautiful sunset I have ever seen. I'm going to draw that tomorrow."

Just then, a large brown ball of branches rolled past them.

"That's a tumbleweed," said Dad. "You'll see a lot of those while you're here. It's made of plants that break off from their roots."

Grandma was waiting at the door with a huge smile on her face.

"I'm so glad you're here!" she said. "Come inside."

Just then, they saw a small bird flick its feathery tail.

"That's a roadrunner," said Gus. "They live here in the desert. They eat lizards, bugs, and scorpions!"

"That's right, Gus. We are likely to see more of them tomorrow," said Grandma.

Gus and Sadie talked to her about school and their friends. After a long day in the car, they were getting sleepy.

"What do you want to do tomorrow?" asked Grandma.

"I want to go on a hike to draw some desert animals," said Sadie.

Gus asked, "But what if we see a snake?" Gus was terrified of snakes.

"Don't worry about that," said Dad, yawning. "We'll wear long pants and hiking boots. And we'll watch our step."

"Now, let's get ready for bed," said Grandma. "We have a big day tomorrow."

After Grandma tucked Sadie and Gus into bed, Sadie wondered if she should have asked for another blanket. The room was a bit cold. Was it the air conditioner? But before she could ask, she fell asleep.

Chapter Two

Covered in Snow!

The next morning, Sadie woke up early. She pulled her covers up to her chin. She was so chilly. *Brrr!*

Sadie was sure Grandma had an extra blanket. She hopped out of bed and put on some socks. On her way to the door, she looked out the window and could not believe what she saw. Everything was covered in snow!

"Gus, get up! Look out the window!" Sadie called.

"What's up?" asked Gus. He rubbed his sleepy eyes and tumbled out of bed.

"You aren't going to believe it, but there's snow everywhere!"

"Jumping jackrabbits!" Gus said. "How do you think *that* happened?"

The Joshua tree outside was covered with snow! There were icicles hanging from its branches.

"I don't know how it happened," said Sadie. "But let's go outside and explore."

The kids rushed to wake their dad and grandma.

"What's all the commotion about?" Dad asked.

Gus pointed out the window.

"Well, I've never seen that before," said Dad, rubbing his eyes.

"How about some hot cocoa?" asked Grandma. "And I think I've got some warm clothes you can wear."

The ground was completely covered with fresh, white snow.

"That sand dune looks like a snowdrift," said Sadie. "And look over there!"

She pointed to some black-tailed jackrabbits nibbling on cactus and leaving footprints in the snow.

"They usually get most of the water they need from plants," said Grandma. "But now, they can get water anywhere!"

They stepped into the snow. It was up to their ankles, but it didn't feel cold to Sadie.

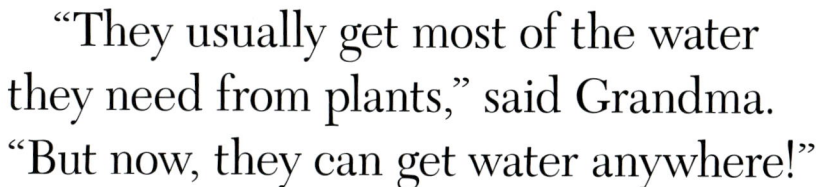

Chapter Three

Building a Snowman

"Hey, look at that!" said Gus.

Tumbleweeds blew in the wind. They picked up snow and became giant snowballs.

"That sure is easier than rolling our own snowballs," said Gus. He pushed the snowy tumbleweeds together.

"Let's build a snowman!" he said. Then, he looked around, worried. "Do you see any snakes, Sadie?" he asked.

"You don't have to worry about snakes in this weather," said Grandma. "They stay underground and hibernate. Some of them sleep in dens, and others find shelter under buildings."

Suddenly, a strong wind began to blow. Large snowflakes were falling. Some were as big as Sadie's head.

"Dad, is this normal for snow?" asked Gus.

"Not any snow that I've seen," said Dad.

The wind was so strong that some of the animals started to blow away. The head of Gus's new snowman rolled right off! The family held on to one another to stay safe and warm.

Sadie saw a family of roadrunners huddling next to a rock for warmth.

One of them looked up and said, "Hi, Sadie! What do you think of our desert home?"

Roadrunners can't talk, thought Sadie. *Can this be real?*

Chapter Four

A Crazy Dream

Just then, Sadie woke up in bed. She looked around in relief. That was one crazy dream! The chill in the room was from the air conditioning, not a snow storm.

She looked outside and saw the sun rising over sand, not snow.

"Hey Gus, get up! We have a lot of exploring to do today."

Sadie slipped into her boots and grabbed her sketch pad and colored pencils.

As soon as they got outside, Gus asked, "How did those tumbleweeds get stacked up that way? They look like a snowman."

Dad followed them out the door. "That looks like the roadrunner we saw yesterday," said Dad.

"Wow!" Sadie said. "How fast can it run?"

"They run faster than you can," Dad said. "You wouldn't be able to catch up to it. They're too quick!"

"Why do you suppose they run so fast?" asked Grandma.

"To catch their breakfast, of course," said Gus. "I'm ready for breakfast too."

"Can I get you some lizards, bugs, or scorpions?" asked Grandma.

Gus made a face. "No, thanks. I'll stick with pancakes and eggs. Yum!"

"That sounds great," said Grandma as she headed inside. "Let's get that pancake batter started."

Gus and Dad followed Grandma inside, but Sadie stayed outside. She sat on the porch and sketched everything she saw today in the desert and last night in her dreams.

About Us

The Author
Ann Ingalls is a children's author and former teacher. She has written over 60 books for young readers. She lives in Missouri with her husband.

The Illustrator
Chris Vallo lives with his wife and two talented children near Columbus, Ohio. In his spare time, he also designs sets for local theaters.

Book Club Questions

1. Predict what might happen next at Grandma's house. What parts of the story help you make predictions?

2. What plants do Sadie and Gus see in the desert?

3. What is the most important part of the story? Why?

4. How might you record a visit to the Mojave Desert? Would you write about it or share it with art? Why?

Sand and Snow

Sadie and Gus go to visit Grandma at her home in the Mojave Desert. They are excited to explore a new place. But the next day, they wake up to a big surprise!

Reading Levels
Guided Reading: L
DRA Level: 24
Lexile® Level: 540L

TCM Teacher Created Materials

120794